The Witch's Lamp

The Witch's Lamp

by

EDITH SNYDER PEDERSEN

MOODY PRESS

CHICAGO

Printed in the United States of America

Contents

1

A Lesson, Dictionary, and Prayer

TEDDY LAY VERY STILL in her soft bed, seeing nothing, even though the red and blue DRUGS sign just outside her bedroom window lit up the room with a friendly glow. She stared at the ceiling, thinking, thinking, thinking.

Her father had come home from a business trip a short while ago. He had come into her room, kissed her on the forehead, and asked, "How are you, Theodora?" When she had said, "I'm fine, thank you, Daddy. How are you?" he had replied, "Oh, pretty well, thank you."

She was in the shadow but then the light was shining in just where he stood. She had seen that he was displeased, even angry. He had said, "Good night, Theodora," and had left the room.

He had not even asked where Mother was. But he had known that she was not at home. Teddy could tell that by the expression on his face, and she felt afraid. The last time he had come home unexpectedly and found Mother gone, he had said, "The next time this happens, there's going to be a separation."

Teddy's throat ached, and something tight and big and lonely filled her chest; she didn't know what to do. Ann Arneson's mother and father were separated. Ann spent half the year with her mother and the other half with her father. Every time she got used to being in one school and made friends, she had to leave them. She hated doing that, and she cried sometimes because her mother and father were separated.

Teddy grew frightened at the thought that she might not see Mother for six months at a time. And she got a lonely feeling when she thought of not seeing Daddy. She loved them both very much.

Her father was tall, and he had brown hair and gray eyes like hers. He was always well groomed and wore nice clothes. He was an attorney and was brilliant, Teddy had heard her mother say.

Teddy was very proud of him. He had a wonderful voice and she was sure he could sing well. But he never did sing; he was too serious for that.

Teddy's mother was beautiful. She had blonde hair, and her eyes were brown. She almost looked—and sometimes acted—like a child. Many times when Daddy was angry, she would look at him just like a little girl getting a scolding. Then Daddy would sigh and stop scolding, and Mother would be very good for a while.

Teddy's mother laughed a lot, especially when she was talking over the telephone. And she sang too. Teddy liked to come home from school and hear her mother singing. But that did not happen very often, because her mother seldom was home when she came from school.

Sometimes Mother's friends, Jane and Mary and Betty, were visiting her. Jane lived in the same apartment building, and her husband was out of town most of the time. Whenever Daddy worked late or went on a business trip, Jane and

Mother would go out with Mary and Betty. Or they would all go to Jane's apartment and play bridge. Once in a while, but not very often, they came to their apartment. But they laughed so loud and made so much noise that they decided it was better not to meet there because they kept Teddy awake.

Jane and Mary didn't have any children, and Betty's children were teenaged, so she said she was not "tied down" with youngsters.

Teddy felt bad because she tied her mother down. She wished she could explain to Daddy that mothers have to have some fun. She was willing to be alone because Mother was so happy when she was with her friends. Her mother had to go out often and have fun, but Daddy didn't understand.

Many people did not understand. Once some of the fourth-grade girls were talking about how wonderful it must be to have their own keys as Teddy did. Mary Lou said she didn't need a key to their apartment because her mother was always at home to give her lunch and her mother didn't think Teddy's mother ought to trust a child with the apartment key.

Teddy felt bad when Mary Lou said that. Until then almost everyone in her class had acted as if she were older or smarter because she had a key. But after that, lots of them stopped admiring her and began feeling sorry for her. That was one of the worst things in the world. Some kids began to make fun of Teddy, and that was worse almost than being felt sorry for. "Is your mother out *again,* today?" Julie would ask. "Isn't she *ever* home?" Patty would ask, and they would laugh and walk away together.

Teddy thought now, lying in her bed, that it would be wonderful to have a "stay at home" mother. It was such a funny feeling to come into the apartment and hear the clock ticking, "tick-tock, tick-tock, tick-tock." She wondered why it ticked so much louder when she was alone. The rooms always seemed so big, and the lunch her mother left for her didn't seem to taste good. It was strange, because if Mother were there, the same kind of lunch always tasted so good.

Once she had thought, *Maybe my mother*

doesn't love me. Then for a little while there had been a pain in her heart and a lump in her throat. But then she had remembered that her mother had often told her that she did love her.

Teddy was the only child in their apartment building, but right across the street every family in that apartment building had children. After school they all played jump or jacks or other games on the sidewalk. They shouted and laughed and had a lot of fun. Several times Teddy asked Mother if she could go over and play with the children. But Mother said, "Teddy, I couldn't give you permission to cross the street. You might be hurt or even killed. There's too much traffic. And what would Mother do without her little girl? I love you too much, darling, to allow you to take such risks." Didn't that prove that her mother loved her?

Just then a door opened, and Teddy heard voices. Her mother had come home. Teddy held her breath so that she could hear what they were saying, but she could not make out a word. It was just sounds. She *had* to know what they were saying. Teddy knew eavesdropping was listening to other people talk when they didn't know you were listening. It was an awful thing, but she couldn't help it. She had to know what Daddy was saying.

Carefully she got out of bed and tiptoed over to the door to listen.

She heard Daddy say something about disobeying. Then Mother said loudly, "Oh, Ted, I'm tired. Do we have to go over this again? I'm not a child."

Father said sharply, "I spoke to Hinley this morning."

Mother said, "Hinley?" There was a long silence. When they spoke again, it was with low voices, so Teddy could not hear everything. But she did hear that word *separation* again.

Teddy felt like crying. She wished she had a friend—someone to talk to. But she had no friend, and she could not talk to her parents because she wanted to talk about them. Where could she go for help?

Then Mother said loudly and angrily, "A house? Out in the wilderness, I suppose?"

"Yes," said Daddy, "on the outskirts of the city. It's comfortable but unpretentious. The choice is yours, Janet. That house or—separation."

What was an "unpretentious house"? Teddy said the words over and over again, "unpretentious house." She wanted to remember the word unpretentious so that in the morning she could look it up.

No one was talking now. Mother was probably trying to decide. *I hope she decides on the "unpretentious house,"* Teddy thought. All of a sudden she did something she never had done before. She prayed. "Dear God," she said, "You don't know me and I don't know You, but God, please make my mother decide on the house. Please, God, if You can."

"Could I see it?" Teddy's mother asked.

"I'm afraid not," her father answered. "I'll have to rent it first thing in the morning if I want it."

"Please, God," Teddy whispered again, "please make her say *yes*."

"All right, Ted," Mother said. "I'll try it.

After all, I'm a gambler at heart. I'll take the chance. I might like being domestic."

Teddy heard their words dying away and she knew they had gone to their bedroom. Climbing back into bed, she said the word *domestic* ten times. In the morning she would look up those words.

Just as she was falling asleep, she remembered God had answered her prayer. Her eyes opened wide, she looked up at the ceiling. *If there really is a God, and there must be,* she thought, *because He made Mother say yes, He's somewhere up in heaven.* She closed her eyes and whispered gratefully, "Thank You, God. Thank You very much."

When Teddy woke the next morning she felt happy. At first she did not know why, then suddenly she remembered. There was not going to be a separation. They were going to move to an unpretentious house, and Mother was going to try to be domestic.

She jumped out of bed, slipped into her fluffy white robe with pink roses on it, slid her feet into her slippers and hurried over to her desk.

She took the well-worn dictionary from the shelf and looked up the word *domestic*. She found it easily, for it was spelled just exactly like it sounded. She read: "Domestic—belonging to the house or home; pertaining to one's place of residence and the family; devoted to home duties or pleasures."

She read it twice and her face lit up with joy. Her mother was going to belong to the house, the home, the family. She was going to be devoted to home duties. This was the most wonderful thing that ever had happened.

Teddy thought she should have prayed long ago. Ruth at school prayed about everything. She said God answered her prayers. Some of the other children laughed at her, and Teddy had laughed at her too. Remembering now, Teddy's cheeks grew hot with shame. Last night she had prayed and God had answered her prayer. But she wouldn't tell the children at school. Well, she might tell Ruth. But she wouldn't tell what the prayer was. It might be a "reflection" on her mother. Miss Bixley had explained that a reflection on anyone was a remark with blame

attached to it. So Teddy decided she would talk
only to God about this thing because He never
would tell it to anyone.

Now Teddy looked for the word *unpretentious* in the dictionary. But the very page on
which it should have been was gone! That
probably was the page John accidentally had
torn out the day he was teasing her. Now she
needed that page. She just had to know what
an unpretentious house was. She could not ask
Daddy because then he would know that she had
been eavesdropping, and she was ashamed to
tell him. Of course it was very wrong for her to
have listened to their conversation, but she
could not help it. It was funny, though. She
felt as if God were on her side and that He did
not mind; it was as if He understood how very
much it had meant to her.

She prayed again. "O God, could You show
me how to find out what *unpretentious* means?
I want to know so much."

Then the thought came, *un* is a prefix meaning *not*. If she looked up pretentious, then she
would know that unpretentious meant just the

opposite. As she turned the pages she was glad Miss Bixley had taught them that in school. And she was glad God had reminded her that she knew it.

I'm going to listen to every single thing Miss Bixley tells us, she thought. *You never know when you will use the things you learn in school.*

"Pretentious: attempting to pass for more than one is worth; pretending to a superiority not real." That meant that the house would not pretend to be something it wasn't. That was funny! A house couldn't pretend to be something it wasn't. Teddy liked people who did not pretend to be important much better than those who did, so she was sure she would like an unpretentious house too.

It seemed as if she were living in a fairy tale because one good thing after another was happening to her. Her family was going to live in a little house in the country and her mother was going to stay at home. Teddy was so happy that she began to sing. She could only remember one song that had God's name in it, so she sang that, making it a prayer, and changing just one word to make it fit.

> Our Father's God, to Thee,
> Author of liberty,
> To Thee I sing.
> Long may our *home* be bright
> With freedom's holy light,
> Protect us by Thy might,
> Great God, our King.

At seven-thirty her father knocked on her door. "I'm up, Daddy," Teddy said. "I'll be ready in a minute."

She hadn't expected that Daddy would be different this morning, but he was. He said, "Good morning, Teddy," not, "Good morning, Theodora." He looked happy and smiled all the time. He never said she should eat this or that because it was good for her. Each ate twice as much as they usually did. They both reached for the sugar at the same time and then burst out laughing. Right in the middle of the laugh, Mother walked into the kitchen.

"Oh, I'm sorry, Janet," her father apologized. "Did we waken you?"

"No, Ted. I just thought I'd like to tell Teddy about the house while we were together."

"Oh, good."

"Daddy is going to rent a little house on the edge of the city, Teddy, and we are going to move into it on the first of April. I hope you will like it, dear, and that you won't mind leaving your school and your playmates."

Teddy hadn't even thought about that. She felt funny and sick when she thought about leaving Miss Bixley and the other fourth graders. But then she remembered that her family would be together. "Oh, I like it, Mother," she said. "I don't mind leaving anyone, just as long as we are together, you and Daddy and I."

She saw Mother and Father look at each other in a strange way. Mother looked a little bit ashamed, her father a little bit proud, as if he had won something.

Just then, Ann began to call Teddy, so she finished her last gulp of milk, ran for her books, called good-bye and hurried down the stairs to tell the exciting news.

2

The Double Negative and Spelling

MANY TIMES THAT DAY as Teddy sat in her front desk and listened to Miss Bixley, she felt afraid. It happened whenever she thought of leaving this room, Miss Bixley, and her classmates. What would her new school be like? Her new teacher? Would she find any friends near their little house on the outskirts of the city?

She listened while Miss Bixley explained that you could not use a double negative in a sentence. That was not part of the lesson, but John had said, "I don't know nothin' about it," so Miss Bixley took time out to tell the class *"Not* and *no* are negatives. If you use both of them in one sentence, you change the meaning of the sentence and it becomes a positive. John said,

'I don't know noth*ing*.' " She emphasized the
ing because John had not sounded the *g*-sound
at all. "In other words, he said, 'I do not know—'
do not know—what, class?"

"Nothing," sang out a few.

"All right, if John does *not* know 'nothing,' it
means that he *does know* something about it.
He must leave out one of the negative words to
make a true statement. He may leave out the
word *not* and say, 'I know nothing about it,' or
he may leave out the negative *nothing* and say
'I do not know anything about it.' Do you understand, class?"

Of course not everyone did understand. But
Teddy did. It was strange about words. Teddy
understood them so easily. Arithmetic was different. She had to think hard to learn that.

Teddy began thinking about things at home.
She was thinking about their house. No matter
how lonesome she would be for the apartment
building, the buses, the kitten, the geraniums,
the red and green flashing sign, Miss Bixley, and
recess in the school yard, she wouldn't cry and
she'd never tell Daddy or Mother that she

wanted to go back. None of those things, however much she loved them, was as important as the fact that Mother and Daddy would not be separated and that she could live with both of them.

If she did not like the country and the house and the new school, Teddy would never tell anyone, not even God, because she had asked Him to make Mother say *yes* and go. She wouldn't complain to Him if she did not like it. But, the more she thought about it, the more she was afraid that she wouldn't like it.

The last day in the apartment came. The curtains were down, the dishes were packed, the beds were stripped of spreads and linens, and Teddy felt like crying.

She sat on the bed, but she was not used to sitting on an uncovered mattress. From the other room she could hear Mother talking on the phone to Mary.

"I know, Mary," she was saying. "It's worse than being buried alive. But what can I do— you know the other alternative." There was a long silence and then Mother said, "Well, I do

love the game, but after all, it doesn't mean as much to me as Ted does."

Teddy became afraid. She wondered if Mary was trying to get Mother to choose the separation rather than the house. And Mother so often did what her friends urged her to do. Quickly Teddy bowed her head and whispered, "You know me, God, for I've talked to You quite a bit lately. Please don't let Mother listen to Mary. Please get us to the house, God. No matter what it is like, just so we'll be together. Please."

"Well, I don't know, Mary," Mother was saying in that unsure way. "I might get used to it. I do get tired of the excitement, and you know how tense I get. I just want to win, win, win and I so rarely do, you know." Another long silence followed, then suddenly there was the shrill ring of the doorbell and noises in the street below. The movers had come. Teddy's mother had to hang up with a tearful "Miss me a lot, Mary, please."

Teddy breathed a deep sigh of relief as that conversation ended. It was pouring rain and was a dismal day. The dreary, dismantled apartment and the moving made Teddy feel afraid.

Teddy had gone to school in the morning because the moving men were to come in the afternoon. As she had said good-bye to Miss Bixley, the tears welled up in her eyes and she had not been able to hold them back. She had sobbed and Miss Bixley had put her arms about her, patted her head, and told her that she, too, would miss Teddy because she was one of her best pupils. "But you will like your new home," she had said. "You'll have trees and grass and fresh air. I know you'll like it, Teddy. And perhaps someday you will come back to visit. We'll be happy to see you at any time."

The moving men assured Mrs. Treyner that the furniture would be well covered and well protected from the rain. There was nothing at all to worry about.

At last everything was gone. Comfortable in the car, they were slowly threading their way through the downpour and the rush-hour traffic of the city. Teddy noticed that Mother once brushed her eyes with her gloved hand. She wished she knew how to comfort her. Teddy realized that Mother was feeling as sad as she was, but she tried to hide the sadness by saying angry things about motorists ahead and behind her, and finding fault with the way they drove.

Mr. Treyner was at the house waiting for the movers. He had gone early so he would be there when the men came to turn on the electricity and the gas. "I'll have something ready for dinner," he had promised.

Teddy began to feel hungry and she wondered what kind of a dinner Daddy would cook. It seemed strange to think of his getting dinner. He always got the breakfast, but that was different.

After a while there were not many cars, and soon they were riding along the road alone. Occasionally a car passed them going in the opposite direction. It was dark, but Teddy could see that there were not many houses. "It seems lonely," she finally said, "doesn't it, Mother?"

She was sorry the minute she said it because Mother started to cry. She stopped the car and fumbled in her purse for her handkerchief, then she cried and cried.

"Please, Mother," Teddy pleaded, "please don't cry. It isn't really lonely. We just aren't used to it. Please, don't cry." Teddy stroked her mother's coat sleeve tenderly, but her mother cried for quite a while. At last she dried her eyes and took Teddy's hand in hers to squeeze it tightly. "Your father is a good man, Teddy. But there are so many things he doesn't understand. He thinks I don't love you or him just because I like a good time. But I do love you, both of you, Teddy. That's why I'm moving out into this wilderness—to prove it." Then she powdered her nose and started the car. In a short time she slowed down and looked at the street signs. At last she said, "I think this is it, Teddy. Does that sign say Baxter Street?"

It did, so she turned off the paved highway onto a dirt road. There were ruts filled with water down the middle of it. Slowly Mrs. Treyner drove the car down the length of one block and said, "We are just about there. It must be that first house to the left."

3

A New Friend

THAT FIRST MORNING in their unpretentious house was the happiest morning Teddy ever had known. Daddy did not go out at all, and Mother helped him make breakfast. They had a lot of fun doing it and Daddy kept calling Mother "Jan" instead of Janet. They smiled at each other often. Once Teddy even thought she heard Daddy sing part of a song.

Teddy was so grateful to the little house for what it had done that she wanted to see it from the outside. Her things were neatly piled in her dresser drawers, and her books were on the shelves, so she pulled a bright red sweater over her head, quietly opened the front door, and walked out. There she was, outside, just like that. There were no long narrow corridors, no inside stairs, no inner door that you could not open until someone upstairs pushed a button, no little tiny hallway that wasn't large enough for more than two or three people, no outer door that let you out onto a cement sidewalk where people were walking, no busy street with cars whizzing by, trucks thundering along, and big buses roaring past.

This, to Teddy, was like fairyland. Trees, trees, and more trees, great big ones that grew up and up and up so high you couldn't see the tops. The branches moved back and forth, blown by the wind. The bright rain-washed leaves, with the sun shining on them, almost tinkled as they danced.

Teddy took a deep breath as she walked to the very edge of the thick velvety green lawn in front of the house. Then she stood looking at the street. It did not seem like a street at all because there was not a car or bus. Across the road there were more trees. The entwining branches formed an arch along the road. She remembered that Daddy had said that half of that

road belonged to the city and the other half to
the county. Across the road, which was too muddy now for her to cross, stretched meadow after
meadow of lush green grass.

Farther away were clumps of trees. Suddenly
Teddy stopped short, for rising up from among
one of those thickets was a column of smoke. It
seemed to be coming right from the trees, but as
she squinted and searched more carefully she
saw that it was from the chimney of a house. The
house was partly hidden and seemed to lean to
one side and to be out of shape. It looked like
a very old and tired house. Teddy was glad
Daddy had not rented that one.

Teddy turned to look at their own little
house. "You are the nicest home in all the
world," she said, "and you've done so much for
me! You've made Mother domestic, and even
Daddy. Thank you, thank you very much."

She went along the walk that led to the back
of the house. It was made of large flat stones
with grass growing between. She skipped as she
glanced up at the blue sky with sailing clouds.
"I wish all the fourth graders and Miss Bixley

could see it," she said aloud. Then she felt a little lonely. Whom would she have for a friend? She returned to the front of her house.

Suddenly an orange fell from somewhere overhead and dropped at her feet. Startled, Teddy looked up. Was that an orange tree?

Had Miss Bixley been wrong? She had told them that oranges grow only in hot climates. Next she head a voice, a very fine voice, singing with laughter in it: "Did I scare you with an orange from out of the blue?"

"Who are you?" Teddy demanded. "And *where* are you?"

"I'm Tommy," the voice replied, and Teddy saw a boy come shinnying down the tree. He was taller than she was and he had red hair, freckles, and eyes that matched the blue sky. He grinned and said, "I'm Tommy Tucker. I live there." He pointed to a yellow house, the only other house on the block. "I'm your neighbor."

"My name is Teddy," Teddy said.

"That's a boy's name," Tommy answered. "Do you like to climb trees and fly kites like boys do?"

Teddy looked at the tree Tommy had just descended. She could not lie, but she wanted a friend, so she answered, "I'm sure I could if I tried."

"Never been up in a tree, I'll bet," laughed Tommy.

"No," Teddy admitted, "but there weren't any where we lived, only little skinny ones planted in the parkway."

Teddy spied the orange. "Where did you learn that song?"

"Made it up. Always do when I need one. I hardly ever sing other songs. They don't say what I want to say."

"I know it," Teddy admitted. "But you can change the words and make them fit." She was remembering how she had changed "My Country 'Tis of Thee."

"Give me a f'rinstance," Tommy demanded.

"A what?"

"An example. A for instance."

"Oh! Well, I did it only once and I don't want to tell anyone about it."

Tommy studied her for a moment. Then, instead of teasing her to tell as the boys at school would do, he said with comforting finality, "Well, that's that." Anyone could see that he respected secrets. He must have secrets too, Teddy decided.

"Well, I've got to be going," Tommy said. "Got to do our Saturday shopping. Here's the orange, a welcome present for you." He held it ready and then, along with another quick smile, the orange came through the air. Teddy caught it, as Tommy waved and started to run. Suddenly he turned to call, "See you later." Teddy nodded her head in agreement. But Tommy could not see her, for he was running toward the store on the highway. She had the orange he had dropped at her feet. It looked as sunny and sweet as Tommy.

4

A Witch, Violets, and a Disappointment

TEDDY STOOD for a long time holding the big orange in her hand. Tommy was nice. He was fun. Being friends with him was going to be nice.

When Teddy finally went into the house she called, "Mother, Daddy, I've got a friend!"

"A friend?" her mother asked. "Who is she, Teddy?"

"Oh, Mother, Tommy is a boy and he is the nicest boy anyone ever met. He knows so many things and he smiles like—a rainbow."

"A boy! Oh, Teddy," her mother said with disapproval in her voice. "Please don't make friends with anyone until I have met him. It's impossible to know just what kind of people live around us. I thought perhaps you wouldn't need friends. You'll have the yard and so many things you didn't have at the apartment."

Teddy's eyes filled with tears as she said, "Mother, I want to have Tommy for a friend."

"Where does he live, dear? What does his father do? And what kind of home do they have?"

"I don't know anything about his family," Teddy admitted. "They live right down the block in that yellow house."

"Perhaps his mother will call on me and then we'll see, dear, if you may have him for a friend."

"But, Mother—" Teddy began. She just had to make her mother understand that Tommy already was her friend.

"That will do, Theodora," her mother said. And Teddy knew that when her mother said Theodora, her mind was made up and could not be changed. Teddy slowly opened the door and left the house again.

Teddy walked back to a large tree stump that had been left in the yard for a seat. It was dry now, for the sun had been shining on it for a while. She sat down and it seemed as if the sunshine were oozing out of her. What if Mother didn't like Tommy? What would she do?

It seemed strange. An hour ago she had not known Tommy. She had thought she was happy then. Now, just because he might be forbidden, she was sad.

Then Teddy remembered how God had helped her before. She closed her eyes and sat there quietly for a moment. Then she whispered, "You remember me, don't You, God? I asked You to bring us here to this house. And You did. Thank You. And now, God, I don't like to be asking You always for something, but I would like Tommy for a friend. Please help Mother to like him. And, O God, help me to be a good friend to him."

When she opened her eyes she was quite sure that God would answer that prayer.

Tommy's mother did not come to call, but Tommy did, that very afternoon.

He introduced himself to Mr. Treyner when he answered the ring of the doorbell. "Hello,

Mr. Treyner," he stated. "I'm Tommy Tucker
—that is, Thomas J. Tucker—and I live in the
house down the block. I thought I'd better come
over and get acquainted and ask you if there's
anything I can do for you. I could see that Teddy gets to school and home again OK. It's quite
a long way to school and I'd be glad to show her
the way."

Mr. Treyner brought him in and introduced
him to Mrs. Treyner. If she had any plans for
finding out more about his people, she did not
have to use them, because Tommy explained
everything.

"My mother works because my father is
dead," he told them. "She doesn't have any time
for visiting. Evenings she washes and bakes and
does things like that. Of course, I help her. She
gets pretty tired working all day. I don't feel
tired until nine o'clock. My mother appreciates
it when I help her. I even bake." He grinned.
"That's girls' work, I know, but I don't care.
It's fun to do it, and I feel kind of proud when
I eat what I have made."

"Have you lived here for a long time, Tommy?" Teddy's mother asked and, by the tone of her voice, Teddy was quite sure that her mother liked Tommy.

"No, we haven't, Mrs. Treyner. We just moved here last September. But it's a good place to live. I've gained weight and I'm stronger already. It's going to be lots of fun this summer. I'll make a kite for Teddy. Have to make one for myself anyway. Might as well make two."

Teddy beamed with delight while her mother and father laughed. "Well, she's a lucky girl to have a friend like you, Tom," Daddy said, smiling at them. Then Teddy went outside with Tommy to play.

"Before we moved here," Teddy said, "Mother didn't want me to cross the street. But I can cross it here any time without asking. Come on," she challenged, "I'll race you."

The road was slippery although not nearly as muddy as it had been earlier. They had to cross carefully.

"Did you notice that ramshackle house there, almost hidden by the trees?" Tommy asked.

"Yes, I did. Does anyone live there?"

"Sure, a witch," Tommy said as if that were not a strange thing at all.

"A witch?" Teddy gasped. "Oh, Tommy, you're fooling."

"Well, that's what everyone says. The boys walk over there and throw stones and call her names. She comes out with a big stick. Then they run."

"Did you ever do that?"

"No."

"Why? Aren't you scared?"

"No. I mean that isn't the reason. My Sunday school teacher taught us the golden rule."

"What is it?"

"Do unto others as you would have them do unto you."

"Do you always?"

"I try," said Tommy.

"Well, would that count for a witch?"

"My mother said she isn't a witch."

"Tommy, does your mother know her?"

"No, but she said there aren't any witches."

"I wish I could see her. But I wouldn't want her to see me," Teddy said in almost a whisper.

"Don't see how you could."

"Couldn't we just sneak over?"

Teddy wiggled with horrified delight. She wished that John, Larry, and the girls in the fourth grade could see her now. They should just see her living near to the home of a witch. Yes, and having a friend like Tommy!

Suddenly Teddy pointed with her finger and shouted, "Violets!" She ran, fell to her knees, and called, "Just look!" Tommy followed and looked down. There snuggled in the grass were violets, huge, lovely, purple violets. "Let's pick them," Tommy said. But Teddy said, "Oh, no! We're not allowed to, are we?"

"Why not?"

"Well, you can't in the park."

"Well, this is the country." Tommy laughed. "Let's pick a big bunch of them for our mothers."

They set to work. Teddy was thrilled as she found one huge plant after another. Tommy showed her how to pick them with long stems.

They picked some fern and then turned toward home.

As Tommy said good-bye, he added, "I'll call for you at nine tomorrow morning for Sunday school."

"Sunday school? Oh, Tommy, may I go?"

"Of course."

"Wait, I must ask Mother if I may go."

She hurried into the house, and with shining eyes gave the violets to her mother. "Tommy is waiting outside," she said. "He wants to take me with him to Sunday school tomorrow morning. May I go?"

Before her mother could answer, her father said, "No, you may not."

"But, Daddy—"

"I said no. That is final. Tell Tommy, Theodora."

Teddy looked at him with open mouth. He turned from her searching eyes to his newspaper. That meant the matter was settled. Reluctantly, Teddy went to the door and gave Tommy the message.

"OK," he shouted cheerfully. "I'll see you in the afternoon. 'Night."

5

Who Did What?

SUNDAY AFTERNOON Tommy and Teddy walked across the meadow, carefully skirting the witch's house. "Next Sunday is Easter," Tommy said.

"It is?" Teddy questioned.

"You know what Easter is, don't you?" Tommy asked. He asked because Teddy had told him that she never had gone to Sunday school.

"Of course," she answered proudly. "Time to get new clothes."

"Oh, that isn't what Easter really is," he said.

Teddy looked at him. She had thought about the Easter bunny and eggs, but she thought perhaps Tommy was too grownup to think about such things. She had wanted to impress him with the grownup idea about clothes.

46

How glad she was that he spoke again before she had time to mention the bunny and eggs! "Easter is the day Jesus rose from the dead."

Teddy was so amazed. "Who—did what?" she asked.

"Jesus—He rose from the dead. That's why we have Easter. It's the resurrection day."

"Who is Jesus? When did He rise from the dead? I don't think my daddy ever talked of that. He's an attorney."

"Oh, it happened hundreds of years ago. More than nineteen hundred years. Jesus is the Son of God. Didn't you know that?"

"Do you mean the little baby Jesus you see in the cribs at Christmas?"

"Yes. He was born in a manger because there was no room for Him in the inn. Of course the innkeeper didn't know He was God's Son. None of the people knew it. But angels told it to the shepherds, and they knew it. They knew the Saviour was born."

"What does *saviour* mean?"

"Jesus is the Saviour."

"What does that mean?"

"I don't know. We always say Jesus is our Saviour."

"A tiny baby was a Saviour?"

"Well, He grew up. When He grew up, He did miracles—healed people, everything, fed them—five thousand of them with five loaves and two fishes."

"He did?"

"Of course. Then they killed Him. Nailed Him on a cross and He died. They buried Him and in three days He rose from the dead."

"Is it true, Tommy?" she asked. "Is that really true?"

Tommy wrinkled up his nose the way he always did whenever he was thinking hard. "Well, I don't know," he said. "It doesn't seem possible, does it? I believed it until now though."

"If you think of God as being just as we are, then it doesn't seem true. If God is up there in heaven and can answer prayers, well, if He's God, then He's got power. Why wouldn't God raise Jesus, His own Son, and make Him alive again, Tommy?"

Tommy thought a moment. "Yeah, why

wouldn't He? I believe it. Bill told us about it, and he wouldn't lie. He's a swell fellow." Tommy looked over the meadow to the horizon and then said, "If God made us out of dust and gave us life, why couldn't He give life to Jesus, His Son?"

"Did God make us out of dust?"

"Sure. He made Adam and Eve. We were born but we're made of dust too."

"Who told you, Tommy?"

"Bill did. Say, I wish you could go to Sunday school. You'd learn a lot there."

Teddy was silent. She wanted to go to Sunday school and learn more about God, who had answered her prayers. Then an awful thought came to her.

"Tommy," she asked in a squeaky voice, "if I don't go to Sunday school can't I go to heaven when I die?"

Tommy bit his underlip and thought for a long time. Finally he answered, "Bill didn't say you had to go to Sunday school. He said to mind the golden rule."

"To do to others as you would have them do to you?" Teddy questioned.

"Yeah."

"Well, then, I'll mind it," Teddy said. Then she added, "And I'll get there too." She seemed relieved to know that she didn't have to go to Sunday school.

But Tommy ruined that thought when he said, "I'll ask Bill next Sunday, to make sure."

On Monday Tommy walked with Teddy to school. He was in the fifth grade, so they had different teachers. Teddy liked her new teacher. She was young and pretty and she had a pleasant "up and down voice." Her name was Mrs. Lisle and Teddy loved her and her name.

It had been fun to eat lunch with Tommy at school. It was too far away for them to go home for lunch so they brought it to school. At noon they bought bottles of milk, got straws, and sat under a tree. It was like a picnic.

After school, Teddy rushed home. There was no key around her neck to bother with and she was happier than she ever had been. School had been fun, and now Mother was sitting at home waiting for her, eager to hear about her new friends and the new school.

After talking over the events of the day, Teddy went out to play. As she stood on the sidewalk in front of the house, she was so happy that she began to feel a little bit silly. Out onto the road like a clown she walked, putting all her weight on one foot and then on the other, wobbling back and forth. When she reached the middle of the road she stood and actually closed her eyes. She was remembering the street in front of her apartment building where they had lived before. You had to keep both eyes wide open to cross that street. In fact, you almost needed eyes in the back and in the sides of your head to keep from being hit by the cars and trucks and buses. What fun! Living across the street from the country.

She decided to pick more violets. Walking on the green grass was like walking on a pillow. Suddenly a bird flew up in front of her, singing as he went. "A meadowlark," Teddy whispered aloud. "Tommy said they were here. And how pretty he is!" Teddy looked up at the blue sky above her. "Please, God, I want to go to heaven by the golden rule. I'd like to go to Sunday school. It's very important to me."

The days went swiftly by and Teddy and Tommy spent almost every waking hour together. They had so many things to talk about and to do.

But on Friday afternoons Tommy had to help make deliveries for Mr. Hermon, the grocer. The first Friday was difficult for Teddy because on that day when Teddy came from school she found her mother talking on the telephone to Mary. Teddy's heart was sad. She had been happy when they had no telephone, but now there was one in their little house. Mother was talking to Mary just like she used to talk in the apartment. She was saying that she was bored to tears with both the house and the country. Teddy left the house without drinking her usual milk and eating her peanut butter sandwich. She felt lonely and afraid again as she sat down under a tree in the meadow. She didn't feel like picking violets.

But on Saturday her mother was cheery and

gay again. Tommy built a seat big enough for himself and Teddy up in the apple tree and they had a good time all that day. On Sunday she waited for Tommy to return from Sunday school. She wanted to find out whether or not she had to go to Sunday school to get into heaven. She was relieved when Tommy told her, "Bill said he thought the golden rule would be all right for you if your parents don't want you to go to Sunday school."

A week went by and on Friday again, Mother was talking to Mary. Tommy was at the store, so Teddy went to the meadow. With rain the night before there were hundreds of new violets. Teddy began to pick a bouquet and soon forgot everything else. When she finished one patch another caught her eye. The bunch was getting so thick she hardly could hold it. Then she heard a voice—a strange, peculiar voice calling, "Little girl, little girl, would you come here and help me?"

Teddy looked up, and there, not more than fifty feet away, was the witch standing on her rickety porch, with the big stick in her hand.

The scene blurred before Teddy's frightened eyes. Before she knew what had happened, she was running, running, across the meadow toward home. She ran faster than she ever had run before. Her heart was pounding with fear and with the exertion.

Just as she reached the sidewalk she heard Tommy call, "What's the matter? The goblins after you?"

Teddy stood there trembling and gasping for breath. She still held the violets in her hand. She hadn't even dropped them. Tommy waited until she could talk and then she told him what had happened.

"You were close enough for her to talk to you?" His eyes were wide with amazement.

"Yes, oh, yes, Tommy. She was right there in front of me. And I got so scared, I just turned and ran."

"Well, I should hope so," Tommy commended her. "I'm glad you had sense enough to get out of her way. I should have warned you about going too close."

Just then Teddy's father called her. "See you

after supper," Tommy called after her. So Teddy went in to supper, but she didn't eat much. She gave no explanation other than that she just wasn't hungry.

6

A Light in the Witch's House

THE NEXT DAY the sky was ablaze with rose, pink, blue, and purple as the sun set. The air was perfumed with lilacs and filled with the sound of chirping birds. Everything was beautiful. Tommy, sitting silently next to Teddy, was lost in the wonder of it. Teddy was silent, too, but she was thinking of something else.

Suddenly she spoke. "Do you know we haven't really been obeying the golden rule, Tommy?"

Tommy looked at her with incredulous eyes.

"What do you mean?" he asked. "No stones at the witch's house. No walking on people's lawns. No picking anybody's flowers, even when we were tempted. No cookies without permission."

"Read the verse once more," Teddy said. Tommy dug into his overall pocket for his ragged Testament while he looked at her as if she had lost her mind. The Testament opened almost of itself to the right page and Tommy read, slowly, " 'Therefore, all things whatsoever ye would that men should do to you, do ye even so to them; for this is the law and the prophets.' "

"What does it say?" Teddy asked.

"Say, what's the idea?" Tommy demanded. "You know what it says."

"Yes. It says—*do*. It doesn't say *not do*. It says whatever we would want men to do to us we should do it to them. And Tommy, we've been *not doing* whatever we wouldn't want men to *not do* to us."

Tommy looked at her with his mouth open. Then he gave a low whistle. "Say, you're right."

"I know it. We've been doing negatives—we are supposed to do positives."

"Hmm. Then do you suppose that not throwing stones and not walking on people's lawns won't get us to heaven after all?" Tommy looked hastily across the meadow.

"I don't see how it can."

"No. Well, then, what do we have to do?"

Teddy was sure she knew the answer, but she spoke hesitantly. "I—I'm sure I know—what I—have to do."

"What?"

"I'll have to go and call on—the witch—and ask her what she wanted me to do."

Tommy looked at her with serious eyes. "Honest?" he asked. "Do *we* have to do that?"

What a good friend Tommy was! He had included himself. He had said *we* not *you*. It would be so much easier with Tommy along, but she had to be truthful. "You wouldn't have to go, Tommy, because she didn't ask you to help. And you wouldn't expect anyone to just come to you and say, 'How can I help you?' unless you had asked him first. But that's what I would want someone to do to me if I had asked him and so I'll have to go and ask." Teddy's voice was trembly.

Tommy sighed. "I wonder," he said, "if it is true that that's the way to get to heaven."

Teddy knew that just now he was hoping that

it wasn't true. She was hoping it herself but she had to be truthful. "Your Sunday school teacher told you so, didn't he? He wouldn't lie, would he?"

"No."

"Well, then."

Another pause. At last Tommy said, "Shall we go tonight? Right now?"

Soon it would be dark. Teddy swallowed hard for she didn't think that she could go now, when it was getting dark; but if they waited until to-morrow how did she know the witch would still need help? Usually when you asked for help you needed it right away.

"I'll go now if you will," she said.

"OK," said Tommy. "Let's ask God to help us." So they closed their eyes while Tommy prayed, "O, God, please go with us to the witch's house. We're scared. If you'll keep her from hurting us, we want to do to her as we would want others to do to us. We want to get to heaven someday. Amen."

Together they started toward the gloomy house. The sun was almost gone and in the twilight the house looked spooky. They walked across the fields, straight to the little house and stood together near the back steps. The steps were old and one was missing. They looked up at the curtained window. If only she would come out. Teddy suggested, "Maybe we should go to the front door."

They walked around the house through the thick grass and stood looking at the front of the house. There was no porch, nor any front steps. There was a door, but no steps leading to it. Teddy's eyes grew round with fright when Tommy whispered, "Do you suppose that's why we never see her leave? Does she just go out the front door on a broomstick, and sail away?"

Just then there was a light, moving behind the curtains. Teddy and Tommy stood still, frozen with terror. First they saw a bony, wrinkled hand moving with a light, then all at once, behind the curtain, they saw a lamp. She had lit a lamp. It was a tall, old-fashioned chimney lamp. Its top was a round globe with a little hole on top for the chimney to come through. Around the bottom half of the globe were large pink roses with green leaves. Around the top of the globe were little baby pink roses without leaves.

They stood scarcely breathing when they saw the hand reach out again. It turned the gold key so that the light grew brighter. Then the hand disappeared. The light shone across the green grass of the meadow.

It really was dark and Teddy turned to Tommy. "What shall we do? I don't think she needs help now, do you?"

"I don't know," Tommy answered and Teddy could tell by his voice that he was a little afraid.

Across the field came a wonderful sound. Teddy's father was calling, "Teddy, Teddy. Come in right away."

"We've got to go," she whispered and Tommy nodded. Together they ran across the field, stumbling, jumping, hurrying as fast as they could toward their houses.

"See you tomorrow," Tommy called as Teddy ran to her father who was standing on their porch. She threw her arms about him and nestled her head against his big soft coat.

He lifted her high and carried her into their house.

With a big, big hug Teddy kissed her parents good night. Tucked in for the night, she thought again of the witch and the lamp. She knew that tomorrow she and Tommy would go again and call on the witch. Tomorrow she and Tommy would knock on the door—the back door—and see the witch face to face.

7

Just Like a Grandmother

SATURDAY MORNING TEDDY arose at the time she always did on school days. Usually she stayed in bed a little longer, but never too late. Neither she nor Tommy liked to waste time. They wanted to get their Saturday work done so they might have a long day for play. Today was a special day. They had to visit the witch. So Teddy flew about her work.

When Teddy was finished, her mother hurried her out of the house. She had been impatient and irritable while Teddy had carefully cleaned her room. Just as Teddy was leaving she called out, "I may not be home when you get back, Teddy. If I'm not, I'll leave the key in the maple tree," a secret place they had. This was

the fourth time Teddy was to come home to an
empty house. The saddest part was that Mother
had told her never to tell Daddy. "He worries
about you when I go—shopping," her mother
had said, "but we know that you are perfectly
safe with Tommy. Don't tell Daddy, or he may
not allow you to go out after school."

Often when she came home from school Teddy heard her mother talking on the telephone to
Mary or Jane or Betty, so she was sure that
Mother was seeing them again. Teddy had
noticed that the peaceful look had left her
mother's eyes and the tense look had come back.
Teddy hated to be deceitful and she did not like
to have secrets from Daddy. But she could not
disobey. She could not do anything that might
mean—*separation*.

While she waited for Tommy, Teddy looked
at their little white house. "Why didn't you
keep Mother domestic?" she said. "She was at
first."

When they got halfway across the meadow
they stood looking at the old house.

"Let's pray," Teddy suggested. They closed

their eyes and Teddy prayed, "O God, we're going now. Please don't let the witch hurt us. If we can help her, show us. We want to 'do' and not just 'not do.' Help us not to be afraid to knock at her door. Amen."

"Say, I just remembered something!" Tommy said.

"What?"

"I read something about knocking on a door the other day when I was reading my New Testament. Maybe we should read that."

Tommy opened the book and read, "Behold I stand at the door, and knock: if any man hear my voice, and open the door, I will come in."

Tommy wrinkled his forehead. "What does that mean?" Teddy asked. Tommy went to Sunday school. He ought to know. "Who is knocking? At what door?"

"I don't know. Maybe God."

"Well, it's about knocking on a door and that's what we have to do. I guess that's what God means, so let's go," Teddy said as she started to walk.

They hoped, as they neared the old house,

that the witch would come out on the porch, but she didn't. At last Teddy and Tommy stood on her porch, breathing heavily, and looking up at the closed door. Teddy reached out and knocked. It was a little knock—they hardly heard it. Then Tommy tried. His knock was louder, but not as loud as he could knock if he wanted to do it.

"Maybe she isn't home," Teddy whispered. Suddenly the door knob turned and there they were, face to face with the witch.

8

Believing and Trusting — A Coincidence

THE WOMAN DID NOT LOOK like a witch. Teddy thought, *She looks like a grandmother*. Her face was little, her cheeks were pink, her hair was gray and wavy, and her eyes were blue. They had a merry look.

"Good afternoon, children," she smiled. "Can I help you?"

"No, ma'am," Tommy said. "We came to help you."

"To help me?"

"Yes," Teddy replied, "I was here yesterday, and you asked me to help you, but I ran away because I was afraid."

"Oh, yes, I remember. I'm so sorry, my child. I needed some tea. Didn't have a drop in the house. Miss Meldon wasn't coming until this morning. She's been here and I have supplies again. She brought some cookies. Would you like to come in and have a cookie?"

"Oh, no, thank you," Tommy answered quickly. "We just finished our lunch."

Tommy kept his eye on the big stick which the witch was using as a cane. But he didn't like to call her a witch anymore. Then all of a sudden he said, "We thought you were a witch."

"You thought I was a witch?" The little old lady looked surprised. "Oh, my," she said, "is that why the children run away whenever I go out?"

"We thought you were a witch, but Tommy and I live in those two houses over there, the ones you can see. We were scared," answered Teddy.

The kind blue eyes twinkled. "Oh, my, how funny! I never could understand the children."

"We thought you kept the big stick to chase us with."

"My cane! It's just to help me walk. I'm getting old now and I have a hard time getting around without it."

"I'm so sorry that you didn't have tea last night," Teddy said. "I'd get anything for you."

The old lady stepped out onto the porch and said to Tommy, "If you'll just pull that rocking chair out here, I'll sit down for a spell in the nice warm sunshine."

Tommy pulled it out, then she sat down and invited them to sit on a bench facing her. "My name is Mrs. King," she said with a smile. "What are your names?"

"This is Teddy, Theodora Treyner, and I am Thomas Tucker."

"Teddy and Tommy. What nice names! I'm so happy to know you. I hope we'll be good friends. I'd like to know a boy with sturdy legs who could run an errand for me, now and then."

She spoke about how often she had looked across the fields at night at their lighted windows and had wondered about the people inside. She had watched Teddy and Tommy play and had wished that they would visit her. "I even prayed that you would come," she told them.

"Do you pray?" Tommy asked in surprise.

"Oh, yes, indeed. I need my heavenly Father

every minute of every day. I would be so lonely without Him."

"Who is your heavenly Father?" Teddy asked.

"Why, God is my heavenly Father. Surely you know God, Teddy."

"Oh, we know God," Teddy hastened to assure her. "Tommy goes to Sunday school and he knows. That's why we came here, because of our 'get to heaven' verse." Then the story came tumbling out, about "doing unto others" instead of just "not doing unto others," and Teddy's idea that she must help, even a witch, if she ever wanted to get to heaven.

When the story ended there were tears in Mrs. King's eyes. "God bless you, my children, God bless you," she said. "I know God is pleased that you obeyed that verse, because He always is pleased with obedience. But Teddy and Tommy, that isn't a real get-to-heaven verse at all."

They stared at Mrs. King. They could not believe their ears. They had been so sure that the way to get to heaven was to obey the golden rule. Mrs. King had spoken so positively that they never stopped to think that she might be mistaken.

"Well, then," Tommy asked, because it was very important to him and to Teddy, "what is a get-to-heaven verse?" Tommy had pulled out his Testament and sat holding it tightly.

"Oh, there are many verses that show us the way to heaven, Tommy. Turn to John 14:6 and you'll find one."

Tommy found the place and read, " 'Jesus saith unto him, I am the way, the truth, and the life: no man cometh unto the Father, but by me.' "

"The Father is in heaven, children, and there is only one way to get to Him and that is through the Lord Jesus Christ. He is the way. The only way . You know about Jesus, don't you?"

"Oh, yes," Teddy said. "Tommy told me how He died and then rose from the dead. If God was powerful, He could do things we couldn't do. If He couldn't, He wouldn't be God at all. If He wanted to raise His Son from the dead, He could."

"Do you know why Jesus died, Teddy?"

"Tommy said because some soldiers killed Him."

"Roman soldiers. They nailed Him to a cross," added Tommy.

"Yes, they did," agreed Mrs. King; "but don't forget Jesus was the Son of God. He need not have died. He laid down His life willingly for you and me. Read it in Romans, Tommy, Romans 5:8 and 9." Tommy had a harder time finding Romans. The pages there were very clean and they even stuck together. But at last he read, " 'But God commendeth his love toward us, in that, while we were yet sinners, Christ died for us. Much more then, being now justified by his blood, we shall be saved from wrath through him.' "

"Do you understand His love, children? Not fully, I know. While we were yet sinners, Christ died for us. While we were His enemies, He died for us. And so we are justified, that means *declared not guilty* before God, only by—what does it say?"

Tommy looked again and replied, "By His blood."

"That's it," Mrs. King said with tears in her eyes. "There was only one way we could be justified—declared not guilty—that was by His blood. And so He died and shed His blood that we might be made righteous."

"That sure is a get-to-heaven verse," Tommy said. "Because Jesus died and shed His blood, we can get to heaven. Otherwise, we couldn't."

That was wonderful! Teddy thought. If Jesus died and shed His blood for sinners, then she and her mother and her father would go to heaven. She spoke with a little tremble in her voice. "I'm glad. Then, everybody will go to heaven, won't they? Because everybody sins."

"Ah, no," replied Mrs. King, shaking her head sadly. "Because only those who believe in the Lord Jesus Christ will be saved. He died for everybody, that is true. But not all will receive Him as the only one who can save them from eternal punishment. Here are the ABC's of salvation, children."

"Salvation?" asked Tommy.

"Yes, salvation is being saved from sin and

from eternal death, also knowing that we have a home waiting for us in heaven."

"What are the ABC's?"

Mrs. King explained, "A—'All have sinned, and come short of the glory of God.' B—'But as many as received him, to them gave he power to become the sons of God, even to them that believe on his name.' C—'Come unto me, all ye that labour and are heavy laden, and I will give you rest.'

"You see, children, all are sinners, but only those who actually receive Jesus are made sons of God. Only those who come to Him for salvation find peace and rest for their souls."

"I've never received Him," Teddy promptly confessed. "And, Tommy, remember the verse we read before we came here? Jesus knocks on our door, and if we don't open the door, how can He come in and make us sons of God?"

"He can't," said Mrs. King. "And so, if you believe that you are a sinner and that Jesus died for you, then you can receive Him right now, this moment, and He will save you."

"How can we do it, Mrs. King? How?" Tommy asked.

"Just as you would receive anyone who knocked on the door of your home. You would open the door and say, 'Come in.' Now, Jesus is knocking on the door of your heart. If you want Him to be your Saviour and Lord you ask Him to come into your heart. Not as a guest, children, for guests come and go, but as Lord— the one you must obey. Will you do that now?"

"I will," said Tommy.

"I will, too," said Teddy.

And so they bowed their heads because Mrs. King did, and she prayed, "O heavenly Father, hear the voices of these children as they invite the Lord Jesus into their hearts."

Then Tommy said in a husky voice, "Jesus, come into my heart. I didn't know before that I had to receive You. I'm a sinner, so please save me. I want You to be my Lord, and I'll obey You."

And Teddy said, "Me, too, Lord Jesus. I'm a sinner too, and I want You now as my Saviour.

I'm opening the door of my heart. Thank You, Jesus, thank You very much."

Then Teddy and Tommy raised their heads and looked at Mrs. King. Her face was lighted up with joy and so were theirs, although they did not know it. "And now," said Mrs. King, "you are children of God. And because you are believing and trusting in Christ's death on the cross and not in the works which you do, you are sure of a home in heaven, and God is your heavenly Father."

Later when Tommy and Teddy were walking home, Teddy said, "Tommy, why did your Sunday school teacher tell you about the golden rule?"

Tommy blurted out, "He's truthful. He's a swell fellow. He's going to school to learn to be a minister. He comes way out here every Sunday just to have Sunday school for us kids. There's no church near here, and unless our parents took us, we wouldn't have any Sunday school training. That's what he told us. And he keeps the golden rule, the way we used to do it." Tommy thought a while and then added, "He keeps it the new way. Why should he get up early on Sunday and come way out here unless he really was doing what he would want others to do for him?"

"Is Mrs. King wrong?" Teddy asked. "Because you would think someone going to be a minister would know more about the Bible than an old lady like Mrs. King."

They looked straight at each other, trying to figure it out, then they both said at once, "Mrs. King is right, though."

"She *is* right," Tommy continued, "because we received Jesus. Now He is in our hearts. I'm different. Aren't you?"

"Yes, I am."

"Well, that proves that what she said was true. In chemistry or anything like that, if you try an experiment and it works, then you know that formula always will do it."

"Like when your mother bakes," Teddy said. "When she uses the chocolate cake recipe, she gets chocolate cake. When she uses the angel food recipe she gets angel food cake."

"Yes. When we opened our hearts, Jesus

came in just like He said He would. I'm sure that I'm ready for heaven now. I never was before, were you?"

"No, I never was," Teddy admitted. "But now I am. My sins are gone."

"Mine, too," Tommy added with a big smile. They squinted up into the sunny sky as Tommy's kite, trying to dive, was skillfully handled and brought back to peaceful sailing.

"Don't you love Jesus, Teddy?" Tommy asked. "I always have loved Bill, our Sunday school teacher, but I love Jesus more."

"Well, of course. He died for us. Would anyone else on earth do that?"

"Maybe our parents would. My mother—or your mother and father."

"Yes, maybe they would. We are their children. But do you remember what Mrs. King said?"

"What?"

"When we were enemies Christ died for us."

"She did say that, didn't she?"

"Yes. Tommy, I never thought before that I was an enemy, did you? But I can see now that if Jesus was knocking at my heart's door and I wouldn't let Him in, I *was* an enemy."

"Sure," agreed Tommy, "because if anyone knocked at your house you would open the door. You'd let the grocer or a salesman in, or almost anyone, unless you were his enemy, unless you just about hated him, or you were afraid of him."

"I didn't *hate* Jesus," Teddy said, with a frown. "I never hated Him, Tommy."

"I didn't either. Maybe we were too busy or something to listen to Him knock."

"Anyway, we weren't His friends."

"Now we are," Tommy said positively.

"Surely we are," sighed Teddy with a beaming smile. And then the smile vanished and Teddy looked serious. "But that doesn't settle the question, Tommy. Why did Bill—" She hesitated.

"Give me a wrong steer?" Tommy finished for her.

"Yes, a steer that got you on the wrong way."

Tommy couldn't answer that one. He sat chewing on a long piece of grass, thinking about it. Then he said, "There's one way to find out. I'll ask him tomorrow. I'll stay until the other kids have gone and then I'll ask him."

Teddy wished that she could be there when Tommy asked Bill so that she might hear the answer. Her cheeks grew pink and she said, "I'm going to ask Daddy if I can go with you tomorrow. I ought to go to Sunday school now because I am a Christian."

Carefully Teddy planned her approach. She waited until her father was alone in the living room. She had decided that she would prove to her father that God answers prayer, prove that He is real. She tiptoed into the living room and stood before her father. After a moment he looked up from his book with a frown. "Why are you standing there, Teddy?" he asked, annoyed.

"I wanted to produce some evidence, Daddy."

"Evidence? Of what?"

"Of God."

"Teddy, please don't let yourself get entangled with such things. The idea of God is an old-fashioned notion."

"Daddy, I prayed that God would make Mother come to our house. I heard you talking about it and I knew Mother wouldn't want to come, so I asked God to make her want to, and He did, Daddy. Doesn't that prove that He is real?"

"Coincidence, Teddy," her father answered. "Learn to rely on yourself. Run along now."

"But, Daddy, I want to go to Sunday school. Especially tomorrow. Please let me go. I believe in God and I ought to go."

Mr. Treyner took time to lay his book down. Then he looked straight into Teddy's eyes and said firmly, "I shall not give you permission to attend Sunday school. Do you understand that?"

Teddy's cheeks were burning and she felt angry with her father. It was not fair for him to just say it was coincidence. That made her bold enough to say, "*I* don't believe it was coincidence, Daddy. *I* think it was an answer to prayer."

For a moment it looked as if her father were going to scold. Then suddenly, she could tell that he was thinking, because he bit his lower lip and sat silent for a moment. Then he looked at her with his piercing gray eyes and said, "You pray that your mother will value her child above her gambling. When that prayer is answered," he continued, "I'll believe in God."

Teddy looked straight at him. She knew what he meant. "All right, I will," she said, and walked away quickly.

9

Big Words and a Highway Game

ON SUNDAY MORNING Teddy went to call on Mrs. King while Tommy was at Sunday school. Every time she was close and saw Mrs. King smile, Teddy wondered how anyone ever could have thought of a witch. She looked more like an angel.

"What is it, Teddy?" Mrs. King asked. "You seem troubled."

The tears Teddy tried so hard to keep back spilled down over her cheeks.

"Mrs. King, do you think God would answer a very hard prayer?"

"Is anything too hard for Him, child?" Mrs. King smiled. "Jesus said that if two or three agreed about anything He would hear and answer."

"Did He say that? Then, Mrs. King, will you pray with me for my mother? She loves to play cards for money—Daddy calls it gambling. He is very angry with her because she leaves me alone and goes out with friends. Daddy wants her to love me more than the other things she does. He said when that happened, he would believe in God."

Mrs. King suggested they pray then that Teddy's mother would receive Jesus as her Saviour. "When she does that, Teddy," Mrs. King explained, "the love for the other things will go." Teddy's eyes were shining, for she and Mrs. King had prayed, believing.

It wasn't until they reached the foot of the steps that they noticed Tommy and a young man coming across the meadow. Tommy was eagerly pulling him along. Before they reached the steps he explained, "This is Bill, Mrs. King. And this is Teddy. She's the girl I told you about."

Bill shook hands with each of them. "How do you do, Mrs. King and Teddy," he said with a broad smile. "I'm Bill Jackson. I hope I am not intruding, but Tommy asked me a question this morning—one I couldn't answer. He wanted me to come to you, Mrs. King, and have you explain it to me."

"About getting to heaven, Mrs. King," Tommy said. "I told Bill 'doing to others as you would have them do unto you' was a living verse not a getting-to-heaven verse."

"That's right, Mrs. King. Tommy says we gain heaven through Jesus only, because He said, 'I am the way . . . no man cometh unto the Father, but by me.'"

It took time but Mrs. King explained it all to Bill. She quoted what Jesus had said, that you must be born again or you cannot see the kingdom of God. She told him that flesh and blood cannot inherit the kingdom of God but that a man must be born of the Spirit; and the way to be born of the Spirit was to receive Christ.

Bill finally bowed his head and covered his eyes with his hand. Teddy was sure it was to hide the tears. "All these months," he said, "I've been teaching the boys and the girls a lie."

"Because you misunderstood, Bill," Mrs. King comforted.

"But I understand now. I can see that nothing any one of us could do could ever earn heaven. It has to be a gift. I believe right now that through the shed blood of Jesus Christ I have forgiveness for all my sin and I am ready for heaven."

"You look different," Tommy said with a big smile.

"Well, no wonder," laughed Bill. "I am different. I'm not working my way to heaven anymore. At last I know what Jesus meant when He said, 'Come unto me, all ye that labour and are heavy laden, and I will give you *rest*.' "

Tommy's mother called just then, her voice ringing clear across the meadow. Tommy called back, "Be right there, Mom."

They started for home, but Teddy turned back to Mrs. King and whispered, "Don't forget to pray every day for my mother." Mrs. King nodded her promise and Teddy left with a much lighter heart. She believed that God could and would answer that prayer.

Teddy repeated to Mother many of the lessons Mrs. King taught her from the Bible as she visited her day by day. At first Mrs. Treyner was interested in what Teddy said. But as the weeks went by, she grew indifferent and at last almost angry with Teddy. One day she said sternly, "Teddy, you are thinking and talking too much about Jesus. I'm afraid Mrs. King is not a good influence. Unless you change, I'll have to forbid you to see her."

"Oh, but she's good for me, Mother, really she is," Teddy said. "I've never been so happy. I wish you would call on her, Mother. She would love it because she can't get out. She's so thankful now that Tommy and I run errands for her."

Mrs. Treyner really did want to forbid Teddy to go across the meadow to see old Mrs. King. But she herself went out more and more these days, leaving Teddy alone. Now that summer was here, Tommy helped Mr. Hermon more in his grocery store and delivered groceries part of each day. So in one way Mrs. Treyner was glad that Teddy had a safe companion.

But at last the day came when she flared up as Teddy asked her, "Why don't you want to receive Jesus as your Lord and Saviour, Mother? He'll take away all your sin and He'll be such a good Friend to you, too."

With her cheeks burning and her eyes flashing she said, "Theodora Treyner, I am tired of hearing you preaching to me! You were such a good little girl before, and now you bother me constantly. I warned you that I would have to do it and now I forbid you to see Mrs. King. Don't you ever go to her house and don't you ever speak to her again!"

Teddy looked at her mother with unbelieving eyes, and after a moment of utter silence she cried, "Oh, no, Mother. I couldn't live without Mrs. King."

"Well, you'll just have to live without Mrs. King. It seems that you love her more than you do your own mother. The issue is settled," Mrs. Treyner said in a commanding tone of voice that sounded like her husband.

Tears came to Teddy's eyes and then she began to sob. But Mrs. Treyner would not be dissuaded from her purpose. Teddy could not see Mrs. King again.

A few hours after she had sobbed herself to sleep, Teddy awoke to hear Tommy calling. For a moment she didn't know what the sorry feeling inside was about, but then it all came back. With a sigh, she went to answer Tommy's call and found him standing on the sidewalk beside a lovely bright red bicycle. His eyes were shining. Anyone could see just by looking at him that he was very happy. So Teddy tried to forget her own sorrow and feel happy. "Whose is it, Tommy?" she called.

"Mine," he answered proudly. "Mr. Hermon bought it secondhand, although you'd never know it, would you? I'm to use it and pay a little each week. Mr. Hermon said I could get around much faster with it. Teddy, you know all the time I wished on stars and crooked fingers and things like that, I never got it. Last week I began to ask God about getting one. Aren't you glad that God is our Father and that Jesus said, 'Ask, and it shall be given you'?"

"It's wonderful, Tommy. God must love you

very much to answer your prayer so soon. He hasn't answered mine yet."

"But He will someday, Teddy," Tommy hastened to explain. "You know what Mrs. King said about waiting for God to work. We need patience."

Then Teddy told Tommy that her mother would not let her visit Mrs. King again.

"God will answer our prayers, Teddy," Tommy said. "He won't let them keep you from Sunday school and from Mrs. King. He knows how much they mean to you. Let's pray right now, shall we?" He wheeled his shiny bicycle off the walk, then he and Teddy bowed their heads and asked God to change Mrs. Treyner's mind and also that she would love Jesus.

Teddy felt sorry as she watched Tommy ride off on his bicycle. The joy seemed to have left him.

Almost every day Mrs. Treyner left the house in the morning, but she always managed to return before Mr. Treyner did. The days were long and tedious for Teddy. Tommy was gone much of the time. When he went over to Mrs.

King's, Teddy felt an ache in her heart. But she wanted him to go, because he always came back with encouragement from her and the assurance that God would answer prayer.

One hot, hot day in August, Teddy did not know what to do with herself. She couldn't read and she couldn't swing and she couldn't play. She got tired even before she started. It was so quiet in the house and the yard. There just wasn't anyone around and she felt that she must see somebody. She thought about visiting Mrs. King anyway. The temptation to disobey her mother was so great that at last she walked toward the highway some two blocks away. There were people in the cars whizzing by. At least she could stand and look, and she'd play her old guessing game of how many green cars would come along, or how many blue, or how many black.

In the shade of a huge tree Teddy began her guessing game. She was counting the blue cars when suddenly a tire on a passing car just coming along blew out. The car began to bump,

twist and turn. Before she could do a thing it came straight toward her.

The next thing Teddy knew she was looking at someone in white, a nurse, and she was lying in a white bed. The nurse smiled and said, "Are you awake, Teddy?"

"Yes," Teddy said, but her voice sounded faraway and very, very soft.

"Your mother is here and your father, Teddy. I'd like you to say hello to them."

Teddy saw her mother—a blurry mother—and then there was her father, but he seemed different too. And they both looked scared, but they smiled and said, "Hello, Teddy."

"Hello," she said in that faraway voice. "Hello, Mother and Da—" But before she finished it she was asleep.

Although Teddy did not know it, she did not awaken until the next day. That was three days after the hot day she had walked down to the highway. This time when she opened her eyes, her mother and her father were right there at her bedside. She smiled and spoke immediately.

Her voice was a little bit nearer now. "Hello, Mother and Daddy."

"Hello, Teddy," they said, and they looked so glad and so happy. It seemed funny that just her saying hello could make them that happy.

"I'll tell the head nurse," her father said as he hurried away. While he was gone her mother stroked her hair very softly and whispered, "Oh, Teddy, I love you, darling. I love my little girl so very much."

The nurse came to feel her pulse and look into her eyes and things like that. Then she turned to Teddy's mother. "Yes, Mrs. Treyner," she said, "you may tell her. Just the gist, you remember. Tell it gently—no excitement."

She walked away but did not leave the room. Then Mrs. Treyner began, "Mrs. King sends her love to you, Teddy. She wants you to visit her as soon as you can. And I want you to visit her, darling. She's a dear. She introduced me to your Saviour, honey. I accepted Him, so now I belong to the Lord Jesus and I'll never be so mean again. God has forgiven me, Teddy, and I'm asking you for forgiveness too."

Teddy whispered, "Of course, I forgive you, Mother, and I'm so happy." Then she fell asleep again.

In a few days she was able to stay awake almost all day. Only her parents and Tommy could visit her though. Teddy was so anxious to leave the hospital and go home.

At last that happy day came and she went to a home so filled with love and sunshine and gladness that she whispered over and over again, "Thank You, heavenly Father, thank You."

She found out that the big tree had saved her life. The tree had stopped the car, but the car had knocked her over and she had hit her head on a stone. That was the reason she didn't know much of anything for days. And that was why her mother had been so afraid. She realized, when she found out what had happened, that her little girl had been lonely and had gone to the busy highway just to have something to do. And Mrs. Treyner knew that because she had selfishly withheld her companionship and then had forbidden Teddy the companionship of Mrs. King, her daughter had almost lost her life. God had been merciful. He had used her own sin of selfishness to bring her to Himself.

Now there were singing and laughter and company in the little cottage. Bill came over and talked with them, and Mrs. Treyner became friends with Mrs. Tucker, Tommy's mother. Tommy's mother taught Mrs. Treyner to bake cakes and pies.

Sometimes when the phone rang and Teddy heard her mother say, "Oh, yes, Mary," she smiled, for her mother always told Mary about the Lord Jesus. She would tell how different she was and how much she loved her home and Teddy. There were cottage prayer meetings and Sunday school, and now she was far too busy to spend time in the old ways. "Well, Mary, it's a miracle. I'm amazed myself, but I am a new creation in Christ Jesus now. The old things have passed away, all things have become new."

Before long Mother's old friends stopped calling. They would not come to the unpretentious house, although Mrs. Treyner asked them for lunch so that she might tell them more about what God did and was doing in her life.

10

Mrs. King's Lamp Is Duplicated

THE LITTLE SUNDAY SCHOOL was growing by
leaps and bounds when another family moved
into the neighborhood. They found out that
Bill, the superintendent, believed in the Bible
way of getting to heaven so they came too. They
were Mr. and Mrs. Fredricksen and their five
children, two of whom were old enough to teach
classes. Mrs. Fredricksen's mother came with
them; she and Teddy's mother and Tommy's
mother were in an adult Bible class which Mrs.
Fredricksen taught. Mr. Fredricksen taught the
older boys and had picnics for all of them in his
huge backyard. All the Fredricksens and Grandma Jones were nice and friendly.

Teddy had wished that Mrs. King could come

to Sunday school, and when they began having services on Sunday morning with Mr. Fredricksen preaching, Teddy and Tommy began to pray that she might be able to come. They didn't know how God could answer that prayer, because Mrs. King could only walk a few steps at a time, and there was no road to her house and the meadow was too bumpy for her to walk over it. However, they didn't worry about that. God had answered prayer and they knew He could find a way when they couldn't.

On every Tuesday night, Teddy and Tommy and their mothers went to Mrs. King's house. They talked about the Bible and had prayer. They made tea, talked some more, and had a good time together. Teddy and Tommy kept it secret that they were praying for Mrs. King to be able to go to all the cottage prayer meetings as well as to church.

September came and school began, so the days began to be shorter. When they went to Mrs. King's in the evening it was fun crossing the meadow in the dark. They would all hold hands but sometimes one of them would stumble.

Once Mrs. Tucker fell down, but she didn't get hurt so they all laughed.

That night when they saw Mrs. King they knew that something was wrong. Sure enough, when they asked for prayer requests she told them that a man, some important man from the city, had been there. Her little old rickety house had been condemned and she would have to leave. He gave her a month to move.

She smiled, but her lips trembled as she said, "I know my heavenly Father will not forsake me now."

That night they all prayed for Mrs. King, that God would settle the problem. They hardly knew how to pray because if the little house were unsafe, none of them would want Mrs. King to stay there. They did not want her to leave them; they loved her far too much. They prayed that God would take care of her.

They prayed as they always did that Mr. Treyner would come to know the Saviour, and Mrs. Tucker too. Although she always went with them, she admitted she never had taken Christ to be her Saviour. She often prayed, but her prayers were different. They didn't have much joy in them, but always were for things that she needed or that someone else needed.

Going home that night, they were quiet and walked slowly and carefully. Each one was thinking about Mrs. King and wondering where God would find a place for her to live.

As soon as Teddy and her mother reached home, Mrs. Treyner spoke to her husband. "Ted, can't you do something? Isn't it possible to forestall them, at least until the winter is over?"

"And be responsible if the house should go up in flames, or collapse during a storm?"

Teddy shuddered because she actually had felt the house shake when it was windy.

Teddy and her mother looked so serious, but Mr. Treyner laughed. It was an ugly laugh, not pleasant at all. "What are you worrying about?" he asked. "Why don't you just pray about it? Isn't God able to find a place for her?"

Teddy's mother bowed her head, and when she looked up her eyes were peaceful and calm.

"Thank you for reminding me, Ted. Of course He is. We'll trust Him."

"Daddy," Teddy said softly, "one time, remember you said that when Mother valued her child above her gambling you would believe in God. She does now, doesn't she? Won't you believe?"

Mr. Treyner looked at her with surprise and his face grew red.

"I'll give Him one more chance," he said haughtily. "If He provides a home for Mrs. King—other than an institution, that is—I'll believe in Him."

Teddy looked her father right in the eye. "You should keep your word, Daddy, and believe in Him now. Maybe He'll give you another chance."

There was a knock on the door and Teddy answered to find Mrs. Tucker and Tommy standing there. "I did it," Mrs. Tucker said. "After I got home, I went into my room, shut the door and asked Jesus to come into my heart. I know that He's there now. Let's go and tell Mrs. King, or is it too late?" she suggested.

Although it was late for Tommy and Teddy, four people hurried across the meadow again to tell Mrs. King the good news.

While they were gone, Mr. Treyner sat lost in thought. He knew that Teddy was right. He should have kept his promise. Something had changed his wife. She truly was a stay-at-home mother now and she devoted time and love to Teddy. But Mr. Treyner was stubborn. He did not like to give in. He did not like to admit that he had been wrong. "If Mrs. King finds a home," he said earnestly, "if she does, then, I will believe." Even while he said it he felt ashamed of himself. He knew he wasn't being fair. He knew he had no right to say that an institution didn't count. After all, God could place Mrs. King wherever He pleased. *Who am I,* thought Mr. Treyner, *to dictate to God—if there is a God.*

A few days later, Tommy was rushing as fast as he could to get through with his grocery deliveries. They were planning to go to Mrs. King's that night. It was getting dark and he didn't see a stone on the road, so he lost his balance and down went his bicycle and the box of groceries.

Potatoes and apples rolled in every direction! It took him quite a while to regather them and he wasn't sure that he had them all, so he had to go back to the store and have them weighed again. Mr. Hermon replaced the apples with others and assured Tommy it was all right.

With a singing heart Tommy started on his way again. This order was to be delivered to the Fredricksens. Just as he reached their home, he saw a lamp suddenly light up in the side window. It was exactly the same as Mrs. King's lamp. He laughed. "For a second I thought that it was Mrs. King's house." This was an electric lamp. He could tell by the brightness of the light. Then the shade was drawn down and he saw no more.

He took the groceries around the house and explained why he was so late.

Mrs. Fredricksen asked about his mother and they talked for a moment about her conversion. Then Tommy told them about the special visit planned for that night at Mrs. King's.

"By the way," he said, "I was surprised to see a lamp in your side window tonight. I never saw it in your house before. I guess it must be in Grandma Jones' room."

"Oh, yes, Grandma's most prized possession. Why did it surprise you, Tommy?"

"Because it is exactly the same as Mrs. King's, 'cepting that Mrs. King's is an oil lamp."

"I don't think it could be exactly the same," Mrs. Fredricksen said. "It probably is similar."

"No, I think it's exactly like it," Tommy insisted. "Doesn't it have big pink roses with green leaves on the bottom half of the globe and tiny little pink roses without leaves on the top of it?"

"Yes, it does." Both Mr. and Mrs. Fredricksen were looking surprised.

"Well, that's just like Mrs. King's."

"Is hers hand-painted?"

"Yes, I've heard her say many times that her mother painted it and sort of made up the design." Tommy stopped short. "Say," he said, "how come yours is exactly like it?"

"That's a good question, Tommy," Mr. Fred-

ricksen replied. Then he turned to his wife,
"Shall we go now, Ruth?" he asked. "Before
dinner?"

"Oh, yes, we must. Let's say nothing to the
children yet, or to Grandma. But we've got to
look into this, John. We've got to find out what
this means."

"We've an errand to do," they told the children. "But set the table and watch the roast in
the oven. We'll be back before long." They
tied Tommy's bicycle to their car and took him
along.

They parked the car in front of Tommy's
house, which was just about as close as they
could get to Mrs. King's little cottage. Tommy
went in to tell his mother that he was taking
them over to introduce them to Mrs. King. But
Tommy found a note which read, "Come to
Mrs. King's as soon as you wash up. Mr. Treyner is away on a business trip and we have decided to have a pot-luck supper at Mrs. King's.
Love, Mom."

11

Potluck and Surprise

LAUGHTER AND THE GAY CHATTER inside the house could be heard before they started up the steps. When they knocked, they heard Teddy shout, "Oh, that must be Tommy!" Teddy opened the door and gasped in surprise when she saw Mr. and Mrs. Fredricksen.

They walked into the little kitchen and Mrs. Fredricksen said, "We brought Tommy. He was delayed a little and it got so dark."

"Well, how nice! Now you have the opportunity to meet Mrs. King. Mrs. King, may I present the Fredricksens? You know all about each other, but at last you meet." Teddy's mother was all smiles as she introduced them.

Mrs. Fredricksen took Mrs. King's hand. "I'm so happy to meet you, Mrs. King," she said.

"But we have come at an inconvenient time. We should have waited until later."

"Oh, no. Come and have potluck with us," everyone chorused.

Mrs. Fredricksen said. "We have dinner waiting at home. To tell the truth, we came over just for a look at Mrs. King's lamp. Tommy told us what a lovely old lamp you have."

The smile left Mrs. King's face. "Oh, I see," she said graciously. "Well, I'm glad to show it to you, but I never would part with it. My mother painted it for me, and it's all I have left of my girlhood days. I wouldn't want to part with it."

"Of course not," Mrs. Fredricksen assured her. "We didn't expect that. We just wanted to see it."

Mrs. King led them into the little parlor where the lovely lamp was sending a soft light into the room. Everyone was silent. All they could hear was the wind outside as it whistled around the house.

Teddy looked at Tommy. Mrs. Fredricksen walked up to the lamp and gently touched the pink roses on the shade.

"Your mother painted this, Mrs. King?"

"Yes. She loved painting, although she never had time for much of it."

"Who was your mother? What was her name?"

"My mother's name was Rosamond Arving," Mrs. King said with a little trace of pride in her voice. "And a beautiful woman she was!"

"Did you have any sisters or brothers?" Mrs. Fredricksen asked.

"I had a sister, Priscilla. She was eight years younger than I. Then I had a little baby brother, Roland, but he died shortly after he was born, and my mother died soon after that."

"And your name," said Mrs. Fredricksen, "is Dorcas, and you lived in Boston."

"Yes," smiled Mrs. King. Suddenly she stopped. "Why, how did you know, my dear, how did you know?"

"You are my Aunt Dorcas. Your sister Priscilla is my mother. And your mother painted two lamps exactly alike and gave one to each daughter. Isn't that so?"

"Priscilla? You know Priscilla? She is still alive?"

"Sit down, Aunt Dorcas," Mrs. Fredricksen said as she gently pulled the little lady down beside her. "We'd better sit down, I guess, we are both shaking too much."

"Priscilla is still alive?"

"Oh, yes, alive and well."

"Mrs. King," interrupted Teddy, "Priscilla is Grandma Jones. Isn't she, Mrs. Fredricksen? Isn't Priscilla Grandma Jones?"

"She is, indeed. What a blessing is in store for her! She has prayed every day for many, many years that she would find her sister."

The wind howled outside, making the little house shake. Mrs. Fredricksen looked troubled. "Isn't it dangerous?" she asked her husband.

"Oh, not in this wind," he assured her. "But it might be in a severe storm."

"Somebody must take charge of this situation," said Mrs. Fredricksen gravely. "I suggest that we bundle up Aunt Dorcas and take her home with us tonight. We can't keep this news from Mother too long."

Mrs. King stood to her feet, eyes shining and cheeks pink. "I don't understand how it came about, but I'm looking forward to seeing my dear sister again. It will have to be later." Mrs. King now spoke with a firm note in her voice. "I must have some of that roast chicken I have been smelling. Let's have our pot-luck now, then we'll see Priscilla."

Mr. and Mrs. Fredricksen laughed. "You're right, Aunt Dorcas. Grandma is so excitable that she never would eat a bit of dinner if we brought you to her now. We'll go home, have our dinner, say nothing to anyone except that we have a surprise and then we'll come for you."

"Yes, for me and also these dear friends," Mrs. King insisted. "I wish them to be present when I meet my sister."

"Good enough," laughed Mrs. Fredricksen. "We'll see you later."

At first no one thought they would be able to eat because of the excitement. But when they sat down to the good things spread out on the kitchen table, they ate heartily, and talked merrily.

"After Mother died," Mrs. King told them, "we lived with my uncle, a very stern man. We never had good times or any company with young folks. So, when I was in my mid-twenties, I left home. I went to Chicago, bringing with me a few clothes and my precious lamp, planning to send for Priscilla as soon as I could. I wrote often, but she never answered my letters. After a few years, a letter was returned to me saying the addressee had moved, leaving no forwarding address. I wrote then to my uncle and received in turn a letter from a neighbor telling me of my uncle's death and that Priscilla had moved away, presumably to California."

The wind was getting stronger; the little house was shaking more and more, but Mrs. King ignored it. "It's nothing," she said, "it always does that on a windy night."

When the Fredricksens returned, the wind whipped through the open door into the house and tore a calendar off the wall. "It's getting worse by the minute," Mr. Fredricksen said. "Bundle up good and warm, Aunt Dorcas. We don't want you to catch cold."

"How is Mrs. King going to cross the meadow?" Teddy asked thoughtfully.

"I'm going to carry her, child," Mr. Fredricksen replied.

"Who is going to carry my lamp?" asked Mrs. King.

"Your lamp?"

"Yes, indeed. I'll have to have it with me to prove to Priscilla that I am her sister Dorcas."

"I'll carry it," Teddy and Tommy both shouted at once.

But their mothers overruled. "It would be better for Mrs. Fredricksen to carry it. She's a niece, and maybe it will be safer too."

Teddy and Tommy agreed. After all, nothing must happen to that precious lamp, tonight of all nights.

Teddy and Tommy would never forget that trek across the meadow. They kept well ahead of the others, running bravely against the angry wind. Every now and then they would stop and look back. All the grownups were walking carefully. Big Mr. Fredricksen carried little Mrs. King with ease.

Teddy's mother was carrying a large box filled with pictures and little knickknacks that Mrs. King wanted to show her sister. Mrs. Fredricksen, carrying the lamp, looked the funniest of all. It was serious business getting that lamp across the meadow, but she looked funny, holding it out before her and feeling her way over the bumpy field.

At last they arrived at the big house. They laid their wraps on the bed, and Mrs. King slowly, carefully took her lamp and walked into the living room. At that very moment, Grandma Jones walked in through another door. She saw the lamp and said, "Who brought my lamp out here?"

Mrs. King smiled as she stepped up, "This is my lamp, Priscilla."

Mrs. Fredricksen took the lamp from the trembling hands and placed it safely on a table.

"Your lamp?" said Grandma Jones as she confronted Mrs. King. "Your lamp?"

"Yes. You know Mother made one for each of us. You remember that, don't you?"

"My mother made a lamp for me, and one for my sister, Dorcas."

"Yes, I am Dorcas. Have I changed so much in fifty years, Priscilla, that you don't remember me?" Mrs. King put her arms around her and cried, "Oh, Priscilla. God is good to give us to each other in the sunset years of our lives!"

After the meeting there were talking and laughter and questions and answers. They found out that the stern uncle never had given Priscilla the letters Dorcas had written to her. Dorcas thought all through the years that her sister had deserted her. They both cried and when they cried, everyone else cried too.

At last Teddy's mother said that they must go. Mrs. King rose from her chair, "Oh, yes. It is getting late. We'll all have to go home."

"But this is your home," said Mrs. Fredricksen positively. "This is your home now, Aunt Dorcas. You and Mother must not be separated again, you know. Besides, the night is too stormy."

At first Mrs. King wouldn't hear of it, but when her sister Priscilla pleaded with her not to

leave, she could do nothing but consent to stay.
"Come, see my room," Mrs. Jones invited. Teddy and Tommy went and peeked too. They saw a lovely room, gay with brightly colored chintzes and packed with crowded bookshelves.

Mrs. King shook her head. "It's too good for me," she whispered. "I've never lived in such style."

" 'Be content with such things as ye have,' Mrs. King," said Teddy. "Remember, you taught Tommy and me that verse. We've been praying for God to find you a place to live. Now you can't complain."

Out into the stormy night they went, their beloved Mrs. King left safely in the hands of her family.

Teddy awakened next morning to hear her father's voice shouting, "Janet, Janet, call a doctor! Call a doctor! Mrs. King's house has collapsed!"

He rushed out of the house while Teddy and Mrs. Treyner fairly flew to the front window. They could see that Mrs. King's house was a twisted and fallen wreck. "Daddy thinks Mrs.

King's in it," Mrs. Treyner said as she ran to the door to call across the field to her husband.

"He doesn't hear me, Teddy. We'll have to get dressed quickly and go after him. He may get hurt if he starts searching for her." Mrs. Treyner helped Teddy dress and put on her boots. "The meadow must be sopping wet," she explained. "Now, Teddy, listen to me, and do not disobey. Don't go near the house. Stay clear of it. Call to Daddy. Tell him Mrs. King isn't there."

It was a dark morning, but it seemed as if the wind and the rain had swept and washed everything. Teddy looked over at Tommy's house, and there he was coming out of the front door. They sloshed over the wet field trying to talk between gasps. "My daddy is there. He thinks Mrs. King is still there. Oh, Tommy—God got her out just in time, didn't He?"

When they got nearer, Teddy suddenly stopped. "I guess I can't go any nearer. Mother said not to."

"Daddy," she called, but she was so out of breath, it was a very weak call.

"Mr. Treyner!" called Tommy, loud and clear. Mr. Treyner!" Then he whistled, a loud, sharp, clear whistle.

He kept calling but it was strange there was no response, so Tommy said, "You stay here. I'll go around on the other side. I won't go too near."

Teddy stood waiting while Tommy started off. She heard voices behind her and saw that her mother and Tommy's mother were coming across the meadow. A shaft of sunlight came shining down through a rift in the cloudy sky.

Tommy saw the ray of sunshine fall upon a man kneeling in the oozing grass. His head was bowed upon a fallen timber. Tommy hesitated to go on, but he heard the man say, "O God, forgive me. You've proved Yourself to me again and again and I've been so stubborn, so sinful. O God, I need You. I need Jesus. I'll take Him as my Lord and my Saviour."

The man reached for his handkerchief and wiped his eyes. Tommy heard him say, "And, please help me find Mrs. King; please help me to find her unhurt."

Tommy ran toward him now and shouted, "Mr. Treyner, Mrs. King isn't in the house. She's with her sister."

Mr. Treyner turned toward the boy. He looked so confused that Tommy repeated the words.

Just then the others came in sight, and Mr. Treyner called to his wife, "Is it true? Is Mrs. King safe?"

"Oh, yes, Ted. Last night Tommy found Mrs. King's sister. Grandma Jones is Mrs. King's sister. Tommy noticed that Grandma Jones' lamp was exactly like one Mrs. King has. The sisters were reunited last night because of the two hand-painted lamps their mother had given them more than fifty years ago. Mrs. King stayed at the Fredricksens'. God found a place for her —and just in time."

"Now, Daddy," Teddy said with a joyful heart and a trembling voice, "now, you will believe in God and accept Jesus, won't you? You promised you would if God answered our prayers."

"It's too late," Mr. Treyner said. Teddy's

eyes clouded. "It's too late for me to do that, Teddy darling, because I already have done it. Just a few minutes ago, I confessed to God that I know He is real. You and Mother have proved to me God is real. I didn't want to confess that I was a sinner. But I am—you don't even know how great a sinner." He spoke with effort. "I knew Mrs. King's house wasn't safe, so I reported the house to the authorities. I had them condemn the place. You don't know how guilty I've felt about it. Then this morning when I arrived home I saw this house.

"I rushed over here to look for her, but I was afraid of what I would find. I had to pray first before I could expect God to answer my prayer. I had to accept Jesus as my Saviour. And I did, Teddy—I did, Jan. Thank God that He has conquered me."

Mr. Treyner gathered both his wife and daughter into his arms. Tommy and his mother turned away to look at the wreckage of Mrs. King's little house. When they had turned the corner and were out of sight of the Treyners, Tommy looked at his mother and said, "Bill really started something when he started our little Sunday school, didn't he?"

"Yes, he did, Tommy. He may have started the wrong way, but a boy who was sincere and true was used of God to turn many from darkness to light. Oh, Tommy, I thank God for you, my son."

"Tommy, Tommy," called Teddy. "Wait for me."

"Wait for us, Mrs. Tucker," called Mrs. Treyner. While their parents walked together across the meadow, Teddy and Tommy skipped and jumped ahead. As the sun came out in full force Teddy said, "Oh, Tommy, I'm so glad that we found out about God's power, aren't you?"

"Yes, I am," Tommy replied, "because by His power we were made children of God and by His power we'll get to heaven."

"Our mothers too, and my father. I'm so glad that He had the power to make my mother a stay-at-home mother and to make my father a believing father."

"Yeah," agreed Tommy. "He used a stone

and a blowout for your accident to answer prayer."

"He used a stone, too, to upset your bicycle," laughed Teddy, "so that you wouldn't be too early to see Grandma Jones' lamp in the window."

"He can use simple things," said Tommy, "and then they become important."

"Some people are like hand-painted lamps, and God uses them. Some people are like stones on the ground—like you and me, Tommy, but God uses us, too." Teddy was really doing some serious thinking.

"You're right," Tommy replied, "God can use us to show Jesus, the light of the world, to many people, just like He used the stone that upset my bicycle and made me late to show me the lamp in Mrs. Jones' window."

Moody Press, a ministry of the Moody Bible Institute, is designed for education, evangelization and edification.